Lucy's Lab

Nuts About Science

Lucy's Lab

Nuts About Science

by Michelle Houts
Illustrated by Elizabeth Zechel

Sky Pony Press
New York

To Amy Phlipot and her Mr. Bones,
for bringing science to life. —M.H.
For Bun. —E.Z.

First Edition

This is a work of fiction. Names, characters, places, and incidents are from the authors imagina-
tions, and used fictitiously.

Sky Pony Press books may be purchased in bulk at special discounts for sales promotion,
corporate gifts, fund-raising, or educational purposes. Special editions can also be created to
specifications. For details, contact the Special Sales Department, Sky Pony Press, 307 West 36th
Street, 11th Floor, New York, NY 10018 or info@skyhorsepublishing.com.

Sky Pony® is a registered trademark of Skyhorse Publishing, Inc.®, a Delaware corporation.

Visit our website at www.skyponypress.com
Books, authors, and more at www.skyponypressblog.com

www.michellehouts.com
www.elizabethzechel.com

10 9 8 7 6 5 4 3 2 1

Library of Congress Cataloging-in-Publication Data

Names: Houts, Michelle, author. | Zechel, Elizabeth, illustrator.
Title: Nuts about science / by Michelle Houts ; illustrated by Elizabeth
Zechel.
Description: First edition. | New York : Sky Pony Press, [2017]. | Series:
Lucy's lab ; 1 | Summary: While learning about habitats in second grade,
Lucy convinces her school to plant a new tree as a home for squirrels.
Identifiers: LCCN 2017008961| ISBN 9781510710641 (hardback) | ISBN
9781510710658 (paperback) | ISBN 9781510710665 (ebook)
Subjects: | CYAC: Habitat (Ecology)—Fiction. |
Animals—Habitations—Fiction. | Trees—Fiction. | Schools—Fiction. |
BISAC: JUVENILE FICTION / Science & Technology. | JUVENILE FICTION /
Readers / Chapter Books. | JUVENILE FICTION / School & Education. |
JUVENILE FICTION / Girls & Women.
Classification: LCC PZ7.H8235 Nut 2017 | DDC [Fic]—dc23 LC record available at https://lccn.
loc.gov/2017008961

Jacket illustration by Elizabeth Zechel
Jacket design by Sammy Yuen

Printed in Canada

Contents

Contents

Chapter One

No More Squirrels

When I get off Bus 21 in front of Granite City Elementary School, the first thing I don't see is the oak tree. The giant oak tree with branches that spread out like big arms ready to give the world a hug. The *only* tree in front of Granite City Elementary School.

The oak tree was where the squirrels always chased each other up and down the trunk. I know, because I saw it happen every day of first grade. Because the oak tree was right outside the room that used to be my first grade classroom.

Except, now it's not. And no tree means no trunk for squirrels to chase each other up and down. So, the first mystery of second grade is: where did that oak tree go? I'm going to have to talk to the principal about that.

Welcome Back
Granite City
Elementary
School
Students!

The first thing I *do* see when I get off Bus 21 is not a thing. It's a who. And that who is my best friend, Cousin Cora. She's my cousin because her mother is Aunt Darian, and Aunt Darian is my mother's sister.

It's fun having a cousin who is the same age and in the same grade. Today is our first day of second grade, and we got lucky again this year—we're both in Room 2-C. Mom says that at school I should call "Cousin Cora" just plain "Cora," because they might decide that cousins don't belong in the same class. I don't think there's a law or anything, but maybe it's a school rule.

My name is Lucinda Marie Watkins, but I'm only ever called Lucy, so I guess it doesn't matter what Cousin Cora—*plain* Cora—calls me.

Plain Cora is waiting for me by the door.
Except Plain Cora isn't very plain. She's very
pink. Cora is very pink *every* day. Pink skirt.
Pink backpack. Pink shoes. Pink hair thingy.
I'm used to it.

I'm not pink at all. My
favorite color is brown,
because lots of good things
are brown. Like caramel
and chocolate. If you think
about it, brown is a pretty
delicious color.

And not only is brown
delicious, it's interesting.
Like brown worms that
wiggle sideways to move
forward. Who else can do
that? Not me. I tried.

And mud pots are brown.

We saw them at Yellowstone National Park last summer, boiling and bubbling right in the ground.

And tree bark is brown. And it hides a zillion little crawly things.

Except on trees that aren't there anymore.

"What happened to the oak tree?" I ask Cora.

"What oak tree?"

"The one that had the squirrels living in it last year."

"Oh, that one." Cora's shoulders go up to her ears, which makes her look like a turtle. "I don't pay attention to trees or squirrels."

I bet she would if the squirrels were pink.

Chapter Two

Room 2-C

The bell rings and Cora and I speed-walk to Room 2-C. Our teacher, Miss Flippo, has put our names on our desks and above the little open lockers on the wall. Cora's desk isn't near mine. She sits down and talks to the girls sitting around her. My desk is near the front, just where I like it. I take my seat and look at the stack of shiny new books in front me.

"Lucy Goosey's in Room 2-C!"

I hear a voice behind me, but I am not going to turn around. I already know who it is. Stewart Swinefest was in my class in first grade. And now, he's in my class again? How can I be so unlucky?

"Lucy Goosey's in Room 2-C!" he calls again, and all the boys around him snicker.

Miss Flippo claps her hands once to get our attention. "Welcome, Room 2-C!"

Then she tells us all the first-day-of-school stuff. Like that we need a bathroom

pass to "use the facilities" now because we are second graders and second graders are not like first graders. Miss Flippo says our bladders are more mature.

We go over the classroom rules. Room 2-C has a lot of rules, and none of them start with *no*. You have to think about them backward to figure out what you're not supposed to do.

"Use an appropriate voice" means "No yelling."

"Raise your hand when you have something to say" really means "No shouting out answers."

And "Always do your own work" means "No cheating."

I think Stewart Swinefest is going to have a hard time with this backward-rule thing.

Next, Miss Flippo takes us on a classroom tour. Except she's the one doing the touring.

Classroom Rules!

- Always do your best.
- Use kind words and actions.
- Use an appropriate voice.
- Raise your hand if you have something to say.
- Listen to each other.
- Always do your own work.
- Clean up after you're finished.
- Take care of our classroom.
- Keep your hands to yourself.
- Share and take turns.
- Try new things.
- Have fun!

She walks around the room and we just turn around in our seats and follow along with our eyes. She walks to the Book Nook, the Math Corner, the Meeting Place. (It was called Circle Time in first grade. Now that we are second graders, I guess we'll have meetings instead.)

Then Miss Flippo walks to the back of the room. "This year," she says, "you'll become observers of the world around you. You will all become scientists."

Stewart Swinefest blurts out, "I don't want to be a scientist. I'm going to drive race cars when I grow up."

Stewart's already broken a classroom rule—the one about raising your hand to speak. But Miss Flippo either doesn't notice or she's giving Stewart a free pass this time.

"Ah," says Miss Flippo. "There is a great deal of science in racing. You'll love learning about engines and motion."

Stewart frowns. I can't tell if he doesn't believe Miss Flippo or if he just doesn't like to be wrong.

Miss Flippo stands in front of a black table with four stools and a sink with a curvy faucet.

"This is our Science Lab," she says.

Whoa! There was no Science Lab in first grade! I sit up taller to see better.

"When you come to the Science Lab, you need a lab coat . . ." She points to four white lab coats hanging on the wall. "And, although you won't actually be using any chemicals until you're older"—I hear Stewart Swinefest say, "Aw, why not?" but Miss Flippo just keeps right on talking—"you must wear protective eyewear if you're using anything that could get into your eyes."

She points to four pairs of plastic goggles sitting on a shelf by the table.

"Always follow directions carefully. A Science Lab can be very exciting, but sometimes it can also be dangerous."

Everyone in Room 2-C goes *Oooh!* at the same time.

"And, this . . ." says Miss Flippo as she lifts a big black cover off of something large in the corner, ". . . is Mr. Bones." A tall skeleton stands in the Science Lab. His bones and his skull are bright white.

Room 2-C goes wild.

"That's creepy!" shouts Stewart.

I don't think Mr. Bones is creepy at all. I think he's pretty cool.

Miss Flippo claps her hands to get us to settle down. Except we don't. So she reaches down and picks up Mr. Bones's two white, boney hands and claps them together.

Now Room 2-C is really out of control.

I think I'm going to like second grade.

Chapter Three

Old Habits, New Habitats

At lunch, Cora and I sit with some new friends from Room 2-C.

Georgia's from Alabama. She just moved to Granite City, and she says all of her long "i" sounds like the short "o" sound, so when she says "I like to ride my bike," my ears hear "Ah lock to rod my bock." I think I *lock* Georgia from Alabama.

Then there's Carl. He was at Granite City Elementary last year, but not in my first grade class. At lunch, he talks a lot about bugs: beetles, moths, spiders and, his favorite, millipedes. Georgia says, "Ew," but I don't think bugs are gross at all. Once, I watched a millipede scurry across the basement floor. It could run really fast. I bet I could, too, if I had that many legs to run on.

Bridget and Ajay were in my first grade class, so they are old friends.

All anyone can talk about at lunch is Miss Flippo and Mr. Bones and how cool Room 2-C is. Well, that and millipedes.

After lunch is recess, and right after recess we have math, then art, and then we go back to Room 2-C. The first day of second grade is almost over.

"Before you go," says Miss Flippo. "I'd like to explain our first group project."

Miss Flippo tells us that we'll be learning about habitats. "Habitats are homes for living things. Habitats are where living things can find the right kind of food and shelter that they need to live. So, as humans, what do we need to live?"

"Pizza!" says Manuel. "I can't live without pizza!"

Everyone giggles. Miss Flippo agrees that pizza is one of her favorite foods, too.

"Some people eat bugs," Carl chimes in.

"Gross!" says Logan.

This makes me wonder which bugs can be eaten and how they actually taste. I bet they're pretty crunchy.

"What about shelter?" Miss Flippo asks.

Natalie raises her hand. "I live in an apartment."

Ajay's house is on the edge of town, and Bridget tells us she lives in a trailer.

"Think about turtles," says Miss Flippo. "They carry their shelter on their backs."

Then she tells us that we'll be learning about several kinds of habitats: woodland, arctic, rainforest, desert, and ocean.

"Tomorrow," she says, "I'll split you into groups, and you'll begin to research a habitat."

Cora and I look right at each other. I see her cross her fingers for luck. I hope we're in the same group, too.

"After several days of research," Miss Flippo continues, "you will begin to construct model habitats right here in the classroom."

I'm not sure what a model habitat looks like, but it sounds like a lot of fun. I hope I get the desert. It's the only one on the list that's mostly brown.

"Oh!" Miss Flippo jumps from her stool, remembering something on her desk. "You have homework tonight!"

Room 2-C echoes with the groaning sound of twenty second graders. Well, maybe nineteen. I usually don't mind having homework.

"I want to get to know you, and I want you to get to know me," Miss Flippo says as she passes out a worksheet with the words "ALL-ABOUT-ME" across the top. We're supposed to put our names on the trunk. Each branch asks a different question that we have to answer. This should be easy.

"Please complete your tree tonight and be ready to share tomorrow morning," Miss Flippo announces, just as the bell rings.

As I'm putting the ALL-ABOUT-ME Tree in my backpack, I remember I have some unfinished tree business of my own!

Just like always, our principal, Mrs. James, is stationed at the door when all the kids come running out of Granite City Elementary School. She yells, "Use your walking feet!" just like always.

It looks like Stewart Swinefest isn't the only one who doesn't know that means "No running!"

I have to pass Mrs. James on my way to Bus 21. Perfect!

I march right up to her.

"Welcome back to Granite City Elementary, Lucy!" Mrs. James says. She has a big smile on her face and is wearing really big glasses.

"Thank you, Mrs. James. Where's the tree?"

Mrs. James looks all around. "What tree?" she asks.

"The big tree. The one that used to be over there." I point at the first grade wing.

"Oh, that tree." Mrs. James's big smile fades away. "Oak wilt."

"Oak *what?*"

Bus 21 honks.

"Your bus is holding up the line, Lucy."

"But . . ."

HONK!

I run for the bus.

"Oak *what?*" I call again over my left shoulder.

"Oak wilt!" Mrs. James shouts. "Look it up!"

Chapter Four

Aunt Darian the Librarian

When the bus drops me off at home, Dad is mowing the front yard. He stops the mower and I tell him that the squirrels have no place to run now that I'm in second grade and the bones of a tall dead guy are in my classroom and can I please go to Cora's?

He wrinkles up his face like he can't understand me, and then he tells me yes, but be back for supper at 5:30.

So, I take my bike to Cousin Cora's. Cora lives three blocks away, but we never get to ride the same school bus. I ride the country bus because I live on the edge of town, right next to the park. She rides the town bus.

There are three places in Granite City I'm allowed to go without my parents: the park, Cora's, and the library. The park, because it's pretty much in my backyard. Cora's, because it's only three blocks and I don't have to cross a road to get there. And the library, because Cora's mom is Aunt Darian the librarian. And because it's right behind Cora's house.

When I get there, Cora has changed from her pink school outfit into another pink outfit. If *I* were taking off pink, I'm pretty sure I wouldn't put on more pink.

"What do you want to do?" she asks.

"Go to the library."

"Me, too! I want the new Cindy Sparkles book!"

Ick. I don't like Cindy Sparkles. She's pink and purple and very, very fluffy.

"Walk or bike?" I ask.

"Walk. The chain came off my bike last night."

"Bummer. I can probably fix it," I say, but Cora's already skipping down the sidewalk, so I hurry to catch up.

"Do you ever wonder what would happen if you woke up one morning and Granite City was gone and you were in a magical kingdom and you lived in a palace instead of a house and you rode a unicorn instead of a bike?" Cora asks, twirling in circles.

"I don't think so." It's true. I don't think I've ever, not even once, thought about what would happen if I woke up one morning, and Granite City was gone, and I was in a magical kingdom, and lived in a palace instead of a house, and rode a unicorn instead of my bike.

"What would happen?" I ask.

Cora stops twirling. "Well, I don't know."

I guess she has never *really* thought about it either.

"Well," I say, "you would probably have a palace maid to make your bed for you. And you might have a palace cook to make breakfast."

"Oh! Yes!" Cora's spinning again. "And you would have a thousand pink dresses, and a hundred diamond tiaras, and a purple rhinestone saddle for your unicorn . . ."

". . . and it would be hard to decide where to park your unicorn at school because you probably can't just tie him to the bicycle rack," I finish for her.

I'm trying to play along, even though I can think of several other problems with Cora's fantasy world. Luckily, we make it to the library doors before I have to tell her that palaces are usually cold (all that stone) and dark (only candlelight, you know).

"At last!" cries Cora. "We've arrived at the Royal Library!"

As Cora and I walk inside, I tell her what Mrs. James said about the big missing oak tree.

"It wilted."

"What's that mean?" Cora asks.

"I don't know. But I'll find out."

We find Aunt Darian at the circulation desk. She isn't surprised to see us.

"I've been saving some brand-new books
for you two."

Cora and I aren't surprised about that.
Aunt Darian always saves books for us. She
calls it a "perk." A perk is what you get when
you have a relative who works at the library.

"For you, Cora . . ." Aunt Darian reaches
under the desk. She hands Cora the newest
Cindy Sparkles book. It's called *Cindy
Sparkles: Ballerina at Bedtime*.

Cora hugs it so tightly that glitter falls off
the cover. "Thanks, Mom!" She beams.

"And for you, Lucy . . ." Aunt Darian
hands me a book about fossils. Really old,
really cool fossils.

"Oooh, thanks!" I say. "Can I check it out
and take it home?"

Aunt Darian smiles. "Of course you can. But
I haven't cataloged those yet, so why don't you
girls look around, and I'll get them checked in.

Then you can check them out, okay?"

Cora goes straight for the fiction section, and I head for nonfiction.

Trees are what I have on my mind. I sit down at a computer, and a few clicks and taps later, I know it's my lucky day. The library has four books about tree diseases!

The first book I find isn't very helpful, but the second has a chapter for every kind of tree. I find the one on oaks, and what do you know? There's a whole page about oak wilt, the disease Mrs. James yelled to me.

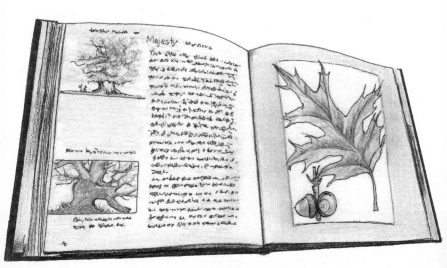

I read until Cousin Cora comes to find me.

"What are you reading about?"

"Oak wilt. What else?"

"Oh." Cora doesn't sound too interested.

"Did you know that a sick tree will lose leaves in the spring or summer? And then it won't grow new ones?"

"Oh, I thought trees only lose their leaves in the fall."

"Those are healthy trees," I explain. "A sick tree loses them early. And a tree can't live without its leaves."

"Why not?"

"Because the leaves use the light from the sun to make food. They need *chlorophyll*. That's what makes their leaves green," I tell her, reading from the book.

"How do you know this stuff, Lucy?" Cora sighs. "You are so smart!"

"I just read it right here." I show her. "I'm

not any smarter than you are."

Cora looks around like she's ready to leave. But I'm not ready. I still have more to tell her.

"Did you know that red oaks die from oak wilt, but white oaks can live longer even if they get it?"

Now Cora looks really confused. "I thought oak trees were green."

"Never mind. I found my answer."

"Well, I don't even know what the question is." Cora sighs.

"The question is: how can we get our squirrels back?"

Cora thinks for a minute. "But why do squirrels need trees at all?"

Her question reminds me of Miss Flippo and our habitat projects.

"For shelter. And protection from predators. My dog, Sloan, always tries to catch squirrels when we go to the park, but they scurry up a tree where they're safe. And squirrels need food, like acorns."

Cora nods. "Speaking of food, how about we go back to our own habitats. I'm getting hungry!" She straightens her invisible tiara and we head for the door. "To the Royal Palace!"

"To the Royal Palace!" I echo.

Chapter Five

The Laboratory

Just before suppertime, Mom comes home from work. She's a teacher at the university. Dad's finished mowing, and he has yummy-smelling chicken on the grill. My little brother, Thomas, is painting on the easel on the back patio. He's four. And most of the time, he's trouble.

"How was your first day of second grade?" Mom asks, joining us outside.

"Room 2-C has a skeleton, the squirrels are homeless, and I'm going to my lab," I say, heading across the yard. I turn and holler over my shoulder, "Call me when dinner's ready. I'm starving!"

"What lab?" Mom asks, but I'm already on my way to the playhouse.

The playhouse is a little shed my dad built when I was small. It's brown and has white shutters and little windows with window boxes that used to hold fake flowers. Inside, there's just enough room for three or four people to sit down on the small chairs Mom got at a garage sale. Mom and Dad can't stand up inside the playhouse—they'd bonk their heads on the ceiling if they tried—but it's still the perfect height for me.

I haven't been inside for a very long time, but it looks the same as I remembered. There's a little kitchen set with a wooden refrigerator, stove, and sink, a little table, and even a pretend telephone hanging on the wall. There are a lot of toys that Thomas has dragged inside. Maybe Thomas needs toys, but I don't.

I need a place to do research. I need a place to solve problems.

I need a science lab just like Room 2-C's.

I push my old play kitchen into one corner. In the cupboard, I find an old blanket, and I use that to cover up the stove and sink. Now I have a research station.

I drag the small table over to one of the windows, placing my new library books on top, and pull some notebook paper and a pencil from my backpack and set them down with the books. There. Now I'm ready to record important observations.

What else will I need in a science lab?

Oh, yes—just like in Room 2-C, if I'm going to keep two eyes for the rest of my life, I'm going to need goggles. I search every cupboard in the play kitchen, but we don't seem to have any goggles lying around. Then I see a solution! One of Thomas's stuffed dinosaurs is wearing a pair of my old sunglasses.

Good enough. I hang my sunglasses/goggles on a hook beside the research station.

And that's all I have time to do before Mom calls me for supper.

Chapter Six

Green Beans and Good Ideas

"Why don't we eat outside?" Mom says. "It's warm, and fall will be here soon." So we sit at the picnic table on the back patio and eat the chicken dad grilled, along with green beans that Thomas won't touch, and a big salad.

"It's good to see you're using your playhouse again," Mom says.

"It's not a playhouse anymore," I tell her. "It's my lab."

Mom smiles. "Well, I think every girl ought to have her own lab if she wants one." She passes the beans to Dad, who nods in agreement.

41

"What's all this about homeless squirrels?" he asks.

Thomas slips a green bean under the picnic table to Sloan. Except Sloan won't eat it. He hates green beans just as much as Thomas does.

I tell Mom and Dad about the tree that isn't there anymore, and about Mrs. James, and about oak wilt. "I didn't see a single squirrel today! Where do you think they went?"

"I'm sure there are plenty of trees around Granite City Elementary School, Lucy," Dad says.

He's right. Behind school, there are a lot of pine trees and bushes and some little maple trees. But not one tree like the giant oak, which had branches that spread out like arms to give the world a hug.

"Dad, those trees are fine, but the squirrels really loved that old oak. They used to run up and down the trunk with acorns in their cheeks. Last year, we could see a nest with baby squirrels in it from my first grade classroom."

Dad looks at Mom and Mom looks at Dad.

"Maybe you can convince Mrs. James to plant a new tree where the old one used to be," Mom suggests.

I hadn't thought of that. *Convince* sounds like a strong word to me. Like maybe it won't be easy to get my principal to plant a new tree.

"How?" I ask. "How do I convince Mrs. James?"

"Well, you have a good reason to want a new tree. That's a start," Mom says.

"Indeed," Dad chimes in. "And a show of public support is always a good thing."

A show of public support? I know what that means! I've seen people on TV marching and chanting to get something they want.

Right after supper I get to work on my signs.

Chapter Seven

Convincing

I pass out signs on the bus on the way to school. I give one to a fourth grade girl named Elizabeth who's wearing a T-shirt that says, SAVE THE WHALES. I figure if she wants to save the whales, she probably wants to save the squirrels, too. Besides, there aren't even any whales in Granite City to save.

I give another sign to Logan, because he asks me for one. I save one for Cora, and I keep the last sign for me. This is *my* Convincing, after all.

The bus stops in front of Granite City Elementary School.

"Follow me," I tell my sign holders. We march right to the two rectangle-shaped windows in front of the school office. "Ready? Now, do what I do."

Logan and fourth-grade Elizabeth and I march in a circle. We shout, "Bring back the squirrels! Plant a new tree! BRING BACK THE SQUIRRELS! PLANT A NEW TREE!"

"What squirrels?" Logan asks. "I don't see any squirrels."

"That's the point," I say. "Keep marching!"

Logan shrugs and starts chanting again. He has a really loud voice.

Lots of kids getting off school buses stop to see what we're doing. When I see Cora, I give her a sign and she joins our circle. More and more kids come over to check out our

Convincing. Georgia, Carl, and Bridget even march with us!

I should have made more signs.

Around and around and around we go in front of Mrs. James's office window.

"How long are we going to—" Bridget starts to ask, but then we see Mrs. James come out of the school's front doors.

"What's going on out here?" Her eyebrows peek up over the top of her really big glasses.

We stop marching.

"I'm having a Convincing." I tell her.

"A what?"

"A Convincing. You know, when you convince someone to do something."

Mrs. James's eyebrows come back down behind her big glasses.

"I see. Would you like to tell me *who* you are trying to convince?"

I smile really big. "You."

Mrs. James doesn't look surprised anymore. "And how about telling me what you're trying to convince me to do?"

I try really hard not to roll my eyes. If she read the signs, she would know. But I don't say that, because the school rule, "Respect others," probably means "Don't be sassy to adults." Instead, I tell her about the squirrels from first grade that aren't here for second grade because the tree from first grade is gone. "It's not fair to the poor squirrels! They need a habitat!"

Behind me I hear, "Yeah!" and "It's not fair!" and "You tell her, Lucy Goosey!"

Ugh. Who invited Stewart Swinefest to my Convincing?

Mrs. James sighs a very big sigh. "Lucy, didn't we talk about this just yesterday? The tree had a disease, remember?"

"Oak wilt. I read about it at the library."

Mrs. James's eyebrows are showing again. And she's almost smiling. That's a good sign!

"You went to the library. Very nice. Then you understand why we had to cut the oak tree down?"

"Yep, I do."

Mrs. James looks like she's thinking very hard. "If you understand, Lucy, then tell me again. Why are you having a . . . *Convincing?*"

I know you have to be very smart to be a principal. But right now, Mrs. James isn't acting very smart.

"Because nobody planted a new tree!"

Mrs. James's eyebrows go all the way up to the top of her head.

"Ready? March!" I shout to my supporters.

Mrs. James jumps into the circle. "No, no! Wait! No need for any more marching."

Logan looks disappointed.

"I have an idea," says Mrs. James. "I'll talk to the PTA about paying for a new tree."

Wow! My Convincing has convinced Mrs. James! That was easy.

"But, first . . ."

Uh oh. There are going to be but firsts?

"I think you young protestors should write reports for me to take to the next PTA meeting. You can title them 'Why Granite City Elementary School Needs a New Tree.' How does that sound?" Mrs. James asks.

Fourth-grade Elizabeth gives her sign back to me. "I'm already working on an essay for Save the Whales. I'm out."

"I just came to yell," says Logan, and then he walks into school.

Stewart Swinefest runs for the door. Most of the other kids quickly follow him.

Cora's still standing with me, though.

"That sounds good to me," I tell Mrs. James. "Cora and I will write our reports this weekend. Won't we, Cora?"

"Yes, we will!"

I smile. Cora's the best cousin ever.

"Good," says Mrs. James. "No more marching, then?"

"No more marching," I promise.

All this, and the day has just started. Not too shabby.

Chapter Eight

A Fine Specimen

Miss Flippo has a great surprise for us in
Room 2-C. The counter by the window near
the Science Lab has lots of new stuff on it.

Except Miss Flippo doesn't like the word
stuff.

"That word doesn't tell us much,"
she says. "*Stuff* can be anything. Food or
clothing or art supplies. Anything at all."

Miss Flippo calls the *stuff* on the counter
specimens.

"Let's define *specimen*," she says as she
looks it up on her computer dictionary so

we can all see it on the screen in the front of the room.

> **specimen** (noun); plural: **specimens**
> an individual animal, plant, piece of a mineral, etc., used as an example of its species or type for scientific study or display.

I decide I like this new word.

The specimens on the long counter look really cool from where I sit. Miss Flippo says there are rocks with little bug fossils in them and a big hornets' nest on a stick. There's even a turtle shell with a crack in it. Miss Flippo says the poor turtle was hit by a truck while crossing the road.

I stretch my neck to see from my seat at the front of the room, but there are too many specimens, and I'm too far away.

"We'll take turns in the Science Lab today," Miss Flippo says. "Everyone will get an opportunity to examine each specimen. You may want to use a magnifying glass, which you will find in the top drawer of the lab table."

Then, Miss Flippo gives us a challenge. I like challenges.

She says that we should look for specimens in nature and bring them in to add to the counter. There's only one rule: living specimens must be in proper containers. That means no creepy-crawly things running around loose.

It seems like forever until it's my turn to go to the Science Lab. I can hardly concentrate on my morning work and my spelling list.

Just before lunch, Miss Flippo calls me, Bridget, Carl, and Stewart to go examine the specimens. I hurry to get there first, remembering the rule about walking feet.

"Put on your lab coat," I remind everyone, and they get the white lab coats off the hooks and put them on. "Put on your safety goggles, too."

But Stewart says, "We don't need safety goggles to examine specimens."

I start to argue with him, when he adds, "Miss Flippo said we didn't."

I put mine on anyway. I like to wear them.

Bridget and I take some fossil rocks and use the magnifying glasses to make the tiny fossils look really, really big!

Except that it's hard to see clearly through the magnifying glass with the goggles on my eyes. I push them up on my head instead. At

least I'm still wearing them.

Stewart is peeking inside the hole in the hornets' nest.

I imagine that there's one little sleepy hornet still inside there, and that it comes out and lands right on Stewart Swinefest's freckled nose! I guess I do imagine things after all. I'll have to tell Cora. She'll be so proud of me.

No hornet dive-bombs Stewart's face. The nest must be empty.

The lunch bell rings way too soon, and everyone lines up at the door. Even me. Except I forget to take off my lab coat and goggles.

"Lucy." Miss Flippo smiles at me. "You look just like a real scientist!"

I grin really big at Stewart. He rolls his eyes at me.

I knew I was going to like this Miss Flippo!

Chapter Nine

Miss Flippo is Out of This World

During lunch, the sky outside Granite
City Elementary School gets dark, and it
starts to rain. Everyone is grumbly about
having indoor recess, but when we get back
to Room 2-C, we see that Miss Flippo has
everyone's ALL-ABOUT-ME Trees hanging
in the hallway.

"There's mine!" Cora points, but she
doesn't have to. Hers is easy to spot. She
has glued pink pom-poms to the end of each
branch. I stop in front of it and read. *Hmm.*
Cora's favorite vegetable is asparagus?

I thought I knew everything about my cousin. Now, here's something I could have guessed: Under "When I Grow Up, I Want to Be," Cora has written "Princess Cora of Granite City."

I look everywhere for Georgia's ALL-ABOUT-ME Tree. I find it beside Stewart Swinefest's. Georgia's favorite color is yellow. Her favorite vegetable is okra. *Okra?* Never tasted it. *Whoa!* Georgia has never seen more than an inch of snow. (Just wait until she sees Granite City in January!) When she grows up she wants to be a surgeon or a pharmacist or a marine biologist.

Stewart's ALL-ABOUT-ME Tree is just what I expected. Favorite way to spend an afternoon: Wrestling with his brothers. Favorite movie: *The Monster That Ate Illinois*. Favorite Book: Don't like to read. When I Grow Up, I Want to be: Rich and Famous.

All About Me!

Pink!

Favorite way to spend the afternoon. Wishing I were living in a magical kingdom riding a unicorn!!

What is your favorite color?

Asparagus!!

What is your favorite vegetable?

When is your birthday? July 8

What is your favorite book? Cindy Sparkles Books!!!

When I grow up I want to be...

Princess Cora of Granite City!!!

Something you probably don't know about me? I can pick up things with my toes!

Cora Brill

Do you have a pet? NO!!!

When I've had enough of Stewart Swinefest, I move on. Bridget was born in New York City. Logan loves the color orange. Ajay's name means *victory*. Carl has a tarantula.

63

I like bugs of all kinds, but I've never thought of having a pet tarantula. Maybe Carl will bring it to school for sharing time. That would be cool.

"Come here, Lucy!" Cora calls. "Look at this."

It's Miss Flippo's ALL-ABOUT-ME Tree. Her favorite color changes with her mood. Her favorite book is *The Giant Golden Book of Biology, An Introduction to the Science of Life.* I'll have to see if Aunt Darian has that at the library. On the branch that says "Do You Have Any Pets?" Miss Flippo has written "2 dogs—Buzz and Sally."

"Read this," Cora whispers, pointing to the branch that says, "Something You Probably Don't Know About Me."

"I have been to outer space," I read out loud.

Cora and I stare at each other.

"There's only one possible explanation for this," Cora says, her eyes huge and round. "Our teacher is an alien!"

Chapter Ten

The Cosmic Truth

Back inside Room 2-C, I stare at Miss Flippo. She's talking about our habitat projects, but all I can do is look at the shape of her head. Could Cora be right? Aliens are from space. Normal people are from normal places. Like Granite City. Or Beijing. Or Mexico City.

I squint to see Miss Flippo better, but I feel like someone else is staring. Out of the corner of my eye, I see Cora squinting, too. Not at Miss Flippo. At me!

"Do you see it?" Cora mouths to me.

"Your group will be based on the habitat I

assign you," Miss Flippo says. She's looking my way.

Cora tries again, not making a sound. "She's an alien, isn't she?"

I give her my best you-better-not-get-us-in-trouble face, but all that does is get Stewart Swinefest's attention.

"What's wrong with your face?" he blurts out.

"Stewart, please remember to raise your hand if you have something to say." Miss Flippo gives him a stern look. "Let's all keep our eyes and ears up front."

Cora turns back toward Miss Flippo. *Miss Flippo does have great big eyes, but—*

"All right, listen for your name, please."

Miss Flippo reads aloud from a list in her hand. Collin, Carl, Bridget, and Sarah are Rainforests. Heather, Georgia, Gavin, and Manuel are the Arctic. Cora gives me a shrug when she's called, along with Ming, Logan, and Eddie to be Woodlands. Jack and Brody cheer when they find out they are Oceans, along with Natalie and Annalisa. Pretty soon, it's down to Stewart, Ajay, Tessa, and me. The good news is we get to be Deserts. The bad news is Stewart Swinefest. He's always bad news.

For the next half hour, we get into our

habitat groups and make a list of questions we want to research. Ajay writes the list down while Tessa and I give him lots of good questions. Stewart just keeps talking about how the desert is full of bones of people who died without water.

"You watch too much television," I say.

Stewart points to Mr. Bones. "Ask him. He'll tell ya."

When Miss Flippo calls the class together again, she tells us more about habitats. "Not long ago, I had the opportunity to visit a place that is not a good habitat for most living organisms. Can you guess where that might be?"

No one raises their hand. Even Stewart doesn't have a smart-mouthed answer.

"The North Pole?" Logan finally tries.

"No," says Miss Flippo, "although it *is* very difficult for humans to live in the polar regions, there are some species that thrive there. And I'm sure our Arctic group will discover and share some of them with us."

All of a sudden, it hits me like a meteor falling right out of the sky.

"Outer space!" I blurt out. My hand was most of the way up when the words came out.

My teacher smiles. "Yes, Lucy!"

Everyone in Room 2-C starts talking at once.

"Shh, class. We have all year to talk about my participation in the Educator Astronaut Project, but right now, we need to line up for music."

This is even better than Cora thought. Our teacher's not an alien.

Miss Flippo's an astronaut!

Chapter Eleven

Welcome to My Lab

After school Cora and I head straight to my lab. I can't wait to show it to her.

She looks around for a minute.

"It's just your playhouse with your play kitchen moved around."

Why is it that if you say the word *queen*, Cora has a wonderful imagination, but if you show her a science lab, she can't see past the wooden refrigerator?

"Well, it isn't quite finished yet. I need specimens. Then it'll look more like a lab."

Cora looks at the sunglasses/goggles and puts them on. I have to admit they look like sunglasses, not goggles.

"Here," I say. "I even have a white lab coat for you."

I hand her one of the white shirts my dad wears when he has to dress up, and she puts it on over her pink shirt. I put one on, too.

"It's kind of plain," she says. "Doctors have their names on their coats. Do scientists?"

I think about it. I don't know if they do or not, but it seems like a good idea. We take the shirts off and use permanent markers and our best handwriting to spell our names above the front pockets. I choose brown and Cora uses pink. When I notice she's adding purple curlicues to hers, I put the markers away.

Then we put our lab coats back on.

"Now, what?" Cora asks.

"Now, we get to work on our report for Mrs. James and the PTA."

"Okay," says Cora. "Only, let's do it together. I'll write and draw some oak trees and you give me the facts."

"That's fine with me."

We sit down at my lab table, and I open up the tree book I got from the library then hand Cora three sheets of notebook paper and a pencil.

"See? My lab has everything!"

Cora nods and takes another look around. "I know one thing your lab doesn't have."

I frown. My lab is perfect! It has everything a scientist needs.

"You don't have a Mr. Bones," Cora says.

Except that.

Chapter Twelve

Good News, Bad News

A whole week goes by after I give Mrs. James the very convincing report Cora and I wrote. When I read it to my mom, she said her university students couldn't have done a better job.

Cora and I used the computer and my tree book from the library, and we found some pretty good stuff—I mean *information*. I was right about squirrels depending on giant, old trees like the one that used to be at the school. Big trees provide shelter, safety from predators (especially predators like Sloan that can't climb), and food. We found out squirrels are nuts about nuts. When the report was finished, I was sure it would earn the school a new tree.

In Room 2-C, our habitat projects are really looking great! On Wednesday, Miss Flippo assigns each group an area of the classroom. The Meeting Place is now the Arctic. The front of the room turns into a rainforest, with vines and even a fake anaconda snaking its way over the door.

Ajay, Tessa, and I start to turn the Book Nook into a desert. On Thursday, Tessa brings in a great inflatable cactus she found at the everything-for-a-dollar store. I have three big zip-close bags of sand from Thomas's sandbox and an old plastic tablecloth so the custodian doesn't throw a fit. Ajay comes in with some great dead weeds that look like tumbleweeds if we roll

them into a ball. So far, Stewart isn't helping much. He brings in some chicken bones.

When I get to school on Thursday morning, Mrs. James and her great big glasses are waiting for me.

"I don't have any signs today," I tell her.

I don't tell her that I've been thinking about holding another Convincing to convince the PTA to hurry up and make a decision about my tree. I mean, the school's tree.

"That's good news." Mrs. James does that sighing thing again. "Actually, I have news for you."

I squint a little. It's something I do when I'm trying to guess what someone is about to say. "Good news? Or bad news?"

"A little of both," Mrs. James replies. "Which would you like to hear first?"

I sigh, too. "Hit me with the bad." My dad always says to take the bad first, so that the good helps the bad not feel quite so bad.

"Well, the PTA has allocated all their funds for the fall to the school Harvest Festival."

"Allo-what?" I ask.

"Allocated," Mrs. James says. "It means the money they have is already spoken for."

Oh, that is bad news. No money means no tree.

"Okay, so what's the good news, then?" I ask

"Well, one of the parents on the Harvest Festival committee is also a member of the Granite City Garden Club. They have agreed to donate a tree to our school."

"Hey, my Convincing worked!" I think my voice is louder than it's supposed to be inside school, but who is Mrs. James going to report me to? She's the principal!

Mrs. James is smiling now. "Yes, and just as you requested in your very thorough report, it will be a white oak."

"Good. Because red oaks die really quickly from oak wilt."

"I know, Lucy. You did the research, and we appreciate that. Thank you."

"You're welcome," I say proudly.

"And," says Mrs. James, "we are planning a tree-planting ceremony tomorrow afternoon. I wondered if you and Cora would like to represent the students at the ceremony."

I think for a long time.

"Will I get to give a speech?"

"No, Lucy. No speeches."

"Okay. I'll do it, but . . ."

Mrs. James's eyebrows show up over her glasses again.

". . . do they have to plant the new tree in exactly the same place as the old tree?"

Mrs. James thinks for a minute. "No, I suppose not. Is there a better place?"

"Oh, yes! It should be planted right outside the windows of the second grade classrooms!"

"Well, Lucy, I'll see what can be done," says Mrs. James. "It's settled. I'll see you tomorrow afternoon at three o'clock, in front of the school."

On my way inside, I have to remind myself to use walking feet. I can't wait to tell Cora about the new tree.

But how do you plant a giant oak tree? It's going to take some mighty big equipment!

Chapter Thirteen

The Tree-Planting Ceremony

At dinner, I tell Mom and Dad and Thomas about the tree and how well the Convincing worked.

"Well done, Lucy!" Dad says.

Thomas makes a loud, buzzing noise, and a piece of broccoli falls over on his plate.

"See what happens when a group of like-minded people peacefully share their opinions in an organized fashion?" Mom asks, beaming.

More sawing comes from Thomas's direction, and another piece of broccoli falls.

"Thomas, what are you doing?" Dad asks.

"Cutting down trees."

"Well, cut them all down, and then eat them all up," Mom tells him. I think Mom knows that's probably not going to happen.

"They're going to plant the new tree tomorrow, and Cora and I get to be the student representatives."

"Wonderful," Dad says. "What will you have to do as the student representatives?"

"I don't know." I shrug. "Maybe run the digger."

Mom and Dad laugh like something is very funny. Thomas cuts down more broccoli.

The next morning, I'm ready extra early. I can't wait to find out how the Granite City Garden Club is going to plant a giant oak tree in front of our school. I'm thinking it could involve a helicopter. Or maybe two.

When I get off the bus, I don't see any large equipment. But I'm not worried. The tree-planting ceremony isn't until three o'clock.

On the way into the building, I notice something on the ground. I walk over to get a closer look. Right in the middle of the grass is a bird's nest. It's small and perfectly round. And it's empty. I pick it up and look toward the sky. There are no trees in front of the building. It must have blown here from the other side of the schoolyard.

I'm so interested in the nest, I don't notice Stewart and Collin standing beside me.

"What's that?" Collin asks.

Stewart answers, even though it's my nest. "It's just an old bird's nest. It's nothing."

"It's not nothing," I say. "It's a specimen."

The boys laugh and run inside. Two weeks into the school year and they still don't get the rule about walking feet.

When I get to Room 2-C, I show my specimen to Miss Flippo, and she says she thinks it's a sparrow's nest, but she can't be sure without seeing some eggs. She says I have a good eye for observation, and I should put it on the counter in the Science Lab. It actually fits nicely there because the Science Lab has been turned into our Woodland habitat.

On my way to the back of the room, I pass Stewart and Collin.

"It isn't *nothing*," I inform them. "It's a sparrow's habitat."

All morning, I glance out the window, but no backhoe yet. And no tree, either. *What's taking so long? Squirrels everywhere are counting on those Granite City Garden people to get that tree planted.* I look at the clock a lot in the afternoon, and finally, at five minutes before three o'clock, Miss Flippo leads Room 2-C out the front doors of the school.

Mrs. James and a man in a green hat are standing beside a little hole in the ground.

When all the kids and teachers have gathered outside, Mrs. James asks for her helpers to come to the front of the crowd. That's me and Cora.

"Welcome to our tree planting ceremony!" Mrs. James announces. "It's a special day at Granite City Elementary School."

Mrs. James may be talking, but my ears aren't listening. Instead, my eyes are looking. *Where's the big tree? Where's the big hole?*

I search the sky for the helicopter that's going to bring the giant oak tree—the giant *white* oak tree—but there are no helicopters.

And then I hear my name.

"Isn't that right, Lucy?"

Huh?

Mrs. James and her big, round glasses are looking at me. Cora is looking at me. The teachers are looking at me. The whole school is looking at me!

Mrs. James sighs her big sigh. "Lucy?"

"Yes, Ma'am."

"It is because of your convincing that we are here today. It was your idea to plant a new tree, yes?"

"Uh, um, yes," I say. "So, Mrs. James, where *is* the new tree?"

The man in the green hat turns around and picks something up off the ground.

"Here's the tree," he says, and I can't believe my eyes. The man with the green hat isn't holding a tree. He's holding a—a—a—plant!

"That's not an oak tree!" I blurt out.

Mrs. James's eyebrows are back.

The man in the green hat chuckles. "Sure it is. It's a white oak seedling."

A *seedling*? A *baby* tree? How are squirrels supposed to run up and down a baby tree? How am I supposed to watch the squirrels from my second grade window run up and down a baby tree?

Then Mrs. James puts the tiny tree in the tiny hole and hands me a tiny shovel.

"Miss Lucy Watkins will now throw the first shovelful of dirt into the hole."

Cora holds the tiny tree steady while I take tiny bit of dirt and scoop it into the tiny hole.

The whole school claps and cheers.

For a seedling.

Can you believe that?

After the ceremony, when the kids from Room 2-C are back in their seats, Miss Flippo calls me up to her desk. She smiles really big at me.

"You did a fine job, Lucy. I'm sure you're very happy to see that new tree."

I shrug. "I guess so."

"You don't sound happy."

"I thought the tree would be bigger. Lots bigger. Big enough for the squirrels to play in."

"Oh, Lucy, it will be. One day, it will be tall and strong and mighty just like the one that was cut down."

"But that'll take a long, long time!"

"You're right. It'll take years. Many years."

I let out a big sigh, just like Mrs. James.

"Well, if I had known *that* I would have asked them to plant it outside of the high school!"

Chapter Fourteen

Finishing Touches

After school, Cora comes over to my house.

"Whoa!" Cora stops in her tracks. "Look at your lab!"

I smile.

"I guess I have collected a few specimens since the last time you were here."

"A few? More like a ton!"

It's true. Since the last time Cora was here, I haven't been able to pass up a rock or leaf or a cricket.

I hand her the white lab coat with her name on it.

She puts it on and I put mine on, too. We both have to roll the sleeves up or our hands would be missing.

We sit at the table and look at all of my specimens.

"What's that?" Cora asks, pointing to a bone I found near the trash can last Wednesday.

"It's from some animal," I tell her. "I think it's probably extinct." Actually, it might be a chicken bone from dinner last Tuesday, but that doesn't sound very scientific. I think about Stewart and the chicken bones he brought for our Desert display. I guess he's just trying to use his imagination.

Cora really likes the three white feathers I found in the park.

"Where do you think this feather came from?"

"Let me examine it," I say.

Just last night, I found a magnifying glass sitting on Mom's desk. I'm pretty sure I've never seen her actually use it, so I borrowed it, just in case I needed to take a closer look at a specimen.

"Hmm," I say. When I put it under the magnifying glass, the little feather looks exactly the same. Just bigger.

"Let me look," says Cora. "Hmm." She pushes her shoulders up to her ears and looks like a turtle. "I think it's from a

mythical bird whose magical powers come from the white feathers that grow straight up on the top of its head."

"Really?" I ask. That must be one amazing magnifying glass!

We spend a whole hour in my lab, looking at specimens and talking about what we should try to find next. I think my lab needs a plant or two. Cora says it needs a pet, besides the cricket in the jar, which I will let loose tonight. Miss Flippo says live specimens are for observing, not killing, so after we observe them, we need to return them to their habitats.

We both agree that a Mr. Bones would be a good addition to my lab, but neither one of us can figure out how to get a skeleton. Come to think of it, how did Miss Flippo get a Mr. Bones?

When Cora has to go home for supper, I head to the garage. In the scrap wood pile, I find a flat board that will work quite nicely for what I have in mind. I borrow a hammer and three nails from the work bench and take everything back to my playhouse. I mean, lab.

I get out the permanent markers and in big, brown letters I write LUCY'S LAB across the board. Then I go outside and nail it right above the door. I've never nailed without Mom or Dad helping me, and it takes longer than I think it should. Finally, I stand back and admire my work. It's a little crooked, but at least no one will ever call my lab a playhouse again.

I step back inside and put the markers on a shelf.

Second grade has started out pretty well.

Miss Flippo is the best teacher ever, *and* she's an astronaut.

Our classroom is filled with habitats for almost every living thing.

There is a new tree for the squirrels, even though I'll be old and almost grown up before it's big enough for a squirrel to climb.

Until then, I'll visit the squirrels in the park. Maybe by the time Thomas is in second grade, there will be a few squirrels running around in front of the school again.

And, there's a science lab in Room 2-C.

Best of all, I have my very own science lab. I look around at my table, my goggles, my books, my specimens, and my magnifying glass. It's absolutely perfect!

Nothing can ruin this very happy moment, I decide. Nothing.

And then, I hear a voice calling from the back door of the house.

"*LUCY!* Your father is missing two of his white dress shirts. Do you know anything about that?"

Whoops.

About the Author:

Michelle Houts is the award-winning author of several books for young readers. She lives on a farm with a farmer, some cattle, goats, pigs, and a Great Pyrenees named Hercules. She writes in a restored one-room schoolhouse. As a second-grader, Michelle begged her parents for a chemistry kit but wasn't quite sure what to do when she actually got it. Lucy's Lab allows her to be the scientist she always wanted to be.

About the Illustrator:

Elizabeth Zechel is an illustrator and author of the children's book *Is There a Mouse in the Baby's Room?* Her illustrations appear in books such as *Wordbirds* by Liesl Schillinger, *The Little General and the Giant Snowflake* by Matthea Harvey, and cookbooks such as *Bubby's Homemade Pies* by Jen Bervin and Ron Silver, as well as a variety of magazine and literary journals. She lives in Brooklyn, NY where she teaches Kindergarten.